PuPPy Club

COCO SETTLES IN

riend to Pluto, and to us all

Sally and Suzy

LITTLE TIGER
An imprint of Little Tiger Press Limited
1 Coda Studios, 189 Munster Road,
London SW6 6AW

Imported into the EEA by Penguin Random House Ireland,
Morrison Chambers, 32 Nassau Street, Dublin D02 YH68

www.littletiger.co.uk

A paperback original
First published in Great Britain in 2023

Text copyright © Catherine Jacob, 2023
Illustrations copyright © Rachael Saunders, 2023

ISBN: 978-1-78895-448-8

A CIP catalogue record for this book is available
from the British Library.

Printed and bound in the UK.

Puppy Club

COCO SETTLES IN

Catherine Jacob   Rachael Saunders

LiTTLE TiGER

LONDON

Chapter 1

"HISS!"

"WOOF!"

"MIAOOOOW!"

"Someone catch Coco!" Elsa yelled above the din, as her tiny puppy tore round the sofa with two huge cats hot on her chocolate-brown tail.

The six Puppy Clubbers were gathered at Elsa's for their weekly meeting, but calm had turned to chaos after Elsa's brother, Milo, left the sitting-room door open. The family's cats Juno and Lupo had darted in, cornered Coco in a pincer movement, and pounced! Luckily, Coco had leaped out of the way, but now everyone was trying to rescue the terrified puppy as she skittered across the wooden floor.

"Grab the cats!" Elsa shouted at Milo.

"I'm trying!" he shot back, finally making a successful grab for Juno.

Then Mum appeared, grim-faced. "What on earth is going on?"

Coco sidled over to Elsa, whimpering. Elsa plucked the tiny puppy up into her arms and cuddled her tight. "It's the cats' fault," she said crossly.

Mum bent down and picked up Lupo, who, now there was no puppy to chase, had stopped to wash her tail.

"Elsa, didn't we agree to keep Coco and the cats apart until they start to get along?" Mum said. "Coco's your responsibility!"

"But—" began Elsa.

Mum held up her hand. "No buts. She's your puppy." She took Lupo into the kitchen and returned for Juno, who was struggling in Milo's arms, before shutting the door behind her.

There was an awkward silence. Elsa blinked away angry tears. She hated being told off in front of her friends. She glared at Milo. "That was your fault! You *know* you're supposed to shut the kitchen door so the cats can't get to Coco!"

Milo snatched up his comic. "I'm sorry, OK!" he said, storming out of the room.

"Oh my gosh, Elsa! Poor you! And poor Coco," Jaya cried, reaching over to stroke Coco's ears.

Arlo held out the tin of cookies he'd brought. "Make you feel better?"

Elsa shook her head.

"Those cats are fast," said Daniel.

8

Willow nodded. "They've really got it in for Coco."

Elsa groaned. This was not making her feel any better.

Harper put her arm round Elsa. "I'm sure they'll get used to her ... eventually."

"Will they?" said Elsa, slumping on to the sofa with Coco on her knee.

"I'm sure they will," said Arlo. "Look, everything's OK now."

"Everything's *not* OK!" Elsa said, her voice breaking with emotion. "Ever since Coco arrived, the cats have been awful! She just wants to be friends but they always hiss at her or swipe a paw, or chase her! That's why we're trying to keep them apart. But it's not working. Mum's so stressed and I'm worried..." Elsa paused, not wanting to voice her worst fear.

"What?" Daniel asked, looking puzzled.

"That she'll send Coco back to Underdogs!" Elsa blurted out. Her eyes started to fill with tears at the thought of having to send Coco back to the rescue centre owned by Jaya's auntie Ashani.

Willow's dark eyes grew wide. "She wouldn't?"

Jaya sat down next to Elsa and patted her shoulder. "You've just got to give it time. After all, this was the cats' home first and now they have to share it with a puppy who's getting all your attention. Maybe they're jealous?"

"Well, they shouldn't be. I love my cats, but Coco needs me – she's still a baby." Elsa fondled Coco's tufty ears. The puppy's eyes were drooping. She was clearly tired after all the drama.

"Perhaps you could try distracting them," said Harper, blowing her thick auburn fringe from her eyes. "Give them a toy when Coco's around."

"Maybe." Elsa sighed. "I have to try something, as this isn't working. For a start, I'm going to make a sign for every door saying: PLEASE SHUT!"

Daniel's green eyes lit up. "How about a stair gate?"

"How would that help?" asked Elsa.

"You could put it across the kitchen doorway," Daniel explained. "Then you could leave the door open so Coco and the cats can see and smell each other without getting too close!"

"We have an old stair gate," said Willow brightly. "I can call home and ask Dad to bring it when he picks me up."

"That would be ace. Thanks, guys,

those are great ideas," said Elsa. "Can we write them down?"

Jaya, who was currently Club Scribbler, reached in her bag for the Puppy Club notebook. She turned to a fresh page and wrote:

Coco and the cats — Operation Friendship

1. Stair gate to keep Coco and cats separate.
2. Posters to remind people (Milo!) to shut doors.
3. Give cats attention too, so they don't feel left out.
4. Distract cats from Coco with toys, etc.
5. Give it time!

"Hopefully these ideas will make things go a bit more smoothly," said Jaya.

"I hope so," said Elsa. "You heard Mum. She's made it clear Coco's my responsibility so I'll have to sort this out by myself!"

"Hey, you've got us too, remember!" said Harper, giving Elsa a friendly nudge.

Arlo grinned. "Exactly! We're here to help."

Willow sprang up. "Operation Friendship is go! Coco and your cats will be best buddies in no time!"

Coco gave a tiny bark as she shifted on Elsa's knee, making everyone laugh. "Thanks, guys," Elsa said, feeling a tiny bit better.

"Right, shall we get on with the meeting?" said Daniel, who was Puppy

Club's Top Dog this month.

It had only been a week since the six friends had taken their puppies home and as the animals weren't allowed to mix yet, they'd agreed to hold club meetings at a different house every Saturday afternoon after they'd helped out at Underdogs.

Together they chorused the Puppy Club promise: "We promise to love and protect puppies everywhere!"

"So how are the other puppies doing?" Daniel asked.

Willow grinned. "Peanut's super cute but he does like to chew *everything*! Dad's slippers are his favourite!"

"Minnie is adorable!" Harper said dreamily. "Though she gets so sleepy. We're lucky if she can get through a ten-minute game of fetch!"

"Dash is the opposite," said Arlo. "We have to force him to rest!"

Daniel laughed. "Teddy's still as greedy as ever. As soon as he's emptied his bowl he's sniffing around for more!"

"Bonnie loves her doggie treats too," said Jaya. "My sisters and I have been practising recall with her but unless we have treats, she ignores us!"

"A pup after my own heart!" Arlo grinned, biting into a chocolate cookie.

Feeling better, Elsa helped herself to a biscuit too. Coco opened one eye and sniffed. "Sorry, Coco, not for you!" she said. "We don't want you to get sick. Talking of which, is anyone else feeling a bit nervous about the trip to the vet next weekend?"

"Nervous?" Willow exclaimed. "No way. The sooner our pups get their vaccinations, the sooner we can have puppy play dates!"

Elsa cuddled Coco tighter. "I guess so. It's just the thought of that big needle!"

The puppies were going to be ten weeks old the following Saturday. The Puppy Clubbers had all registered with the same vet and were taking their puppies for their jabs at the same time.

"Willow's right," Daniel reassured Elsa. "The vaccinations protect the puppies from nasty bugs – once they've had them we can take them for walks and they can mix with other dogs!"

"My vet books say we should wait a week after that before they start mixing," said Jaya. "So that's two weeks today."

Harper's green eyes sparkled. "Then the fun begins!"

"Oh!" Willow cried, leaping up again.

16

"How about we have a puppy party, to celebrate?"

"Great idea!" said Elsa excitedly.

Jaya frowned. "Wouldn't it be a bit chaotic, all the pups chasing round together?"

Willow rolled her eyes. "Jaya, where's your sense of fun?"

"You're right," said Jaya, her face breaking into a smile. "It would be amazing!"

"Of course it would. They'll all be so happy to see each other," said Daniel. "Hey! Ashani could come with Lulu. For a family reunion!" Lulu, the puppies' mum, had been at Underdogs but now she lived with Jaya's aunt.

"Awesome idea!" Arlo cried.

"We can ask her when we go round to see Lulu tomorrow," said Jaya.

"And I'll check with Mum and Dad to see if we can have the party in our garden," said Willow.

Jaya nodded. "OK. Shall we do it on Sunday, a week after their jabs?"

Everyone nodded.

"Maybe we should bake a celebration cake," said Harper.

"Two cakes!" Arlo licked his lips. "One for the pups and one for us! As Snack Supremo, I'll look at recipes."

"And I'll make the invitations," said Harper.

"We could do puppy face paints based on our Puppy Club code names?" Elsa suggested.

"Brilliant!" Daniel said. "I've got some new face paints I can bring."

Jaya looked thoughtful. "How about we make a puppy agility course?"

Willow high-fived her. "Fab idea. I'll help you with that, Jaya." She looked over at Elsa. "Why don't you write one of your poems, in honour of the big day, Elsa?"

Elsa beamed. "I'd love to!"

Jaya picked up her pen and made some notes:

Puppy Club Party

Sunday 6th May, 12 p.m.

Roles:

Jaya and Willow: agility course

Daniel: face paints

Arlo: cakes

Harper: invitations

Elsa: poem

Coco suddenly hopped down from Elsa's knee and began sniffing round the room.

"Uh-oh!" cried Elsa, recognizing the signs. "I think she needs a wee!" She leaped to her feet, picked up Coco and hurried out of the room. As she raced through the kitchen to the back door, Juno and Lupo sat watching from their sunny spot on the windowsill. Coco gave them a playful bark. The cats hissed in reply. Elsa wagged her finger at them. "You two need to be kinder. Whether you like it or not, Coco is here to stay!"

Chapter 2

Elsa was always up early on Sundays
for her swimming lesson, but today she
had set her alarm an hour earlier so she
could spend some time with Coco. With
swimming *and* a trip to Ashani's in the
afternoon, she was a bit worried about
leaving Coco on her own for such a long
time.

Downstairs, the cats were still asleep

on their cushions in the hall. Elsa crept past them and quietly opened the stair gate to the kitchen. Willow's dad had dropped it off yesterday. Elsa lifted a corner of the blanket covering Coco's crate and peeped in. Coco was curled up at the back. Elsa felt a rush of happiness. Would she ever get used to the fact this wasn't a dream? She actually had her very own puppy!

Coco blinked open her chocolate-brown eyes. Elsa unlocked the crate and gently picked up the puppy, rubbing her nose into Coco's soft fur, breathing in the sweet, puppyish smell.

"Did you sleep well?" she whispered, as the drowsy puppy snuffled into her fluffy dressing gown. Then she felt something warm and wet seeping through her sleeve. "Oops!" she laughed. "I should have taken you outside for a wee straight away!"

After Elsa had cleaned up, she and Coco had a game of indoor fetch before breakfast – cereal for Elsa, puppy biscuits for Coco – then she made a start on her puppy party poem, with Coco snuggled on her lap. Elsa was so engrossed in what she was writing, she didn't notice the door open.

Mum appeared, with Juno and Lupo at her feet. "Can't you hear the cats mewing, Elsa? They want to be let in! I guess you haven't given them breakfast?"

Elsa's mouth fell open. She'd forgotten about the cats. "I'm sorry! I…"

Mum raised her eyebrows. "Willow's

dad will be here to collect you soon. Why don't you put Coco in the sitting room while you get ready."

Reluctantly, Elsa left Coco and went upstairs. She'd only just found her goggles when the doorbell rang so she rushed down to give Coco a final cuddle. "I'll be back soon, little one," she said, stroking the puppy's ears.

Mum smiled reassuringly. "Don't worry. Milo and I will look after her. Coco will be fine."

"Morning, Elsa!" said Willow's dad, as Elsa fastened her seat belt. "Now what's all this about wanting to have a puppy party at our house?"

"I... er..." Elsa began, not quite sure what to say.

Willow giggled. "Don't worry, he's only joking! They've said yes!"

Willow's dad grinned. Soon after, they stopped to pick up Jaya, then continued on to Harper's house. She wasn't quite ready, so the girls popped in quickly to see Minnie.

"Come in!" said Harper's mum, as a tiny cream furball flew at them excitedly, her black Minnie Mouse ears flapping as she jumped around in glee.

"She thinks visitors are playmates!" said Harper.

"We are!" Elsa laughed, kneeling down next to Willow and Jaya to fuss Minnie.

"Minnie's a lot smaller than Peanut," said Willow.

Harper nodded. "She was the smallest of the litter, remember!"

After a few minutes, Minnie jumped up on the sofa and curled into a ball!

Harper looked dismayed. "Mum! She's going to sleep again! Do you think there's something wrong?"

"She's fine! Remember, she didn't sleep much during the night – and neither did I!" She turned to the girls. "Harper's dad and I took turns to sleep on the sofa next to Minnie's crate as she was whimpering."

Harper still looked worried as they headed out to Willow's car. "Minnie's so

26

tiny. I hope nothing's wrong."

"She looks perfect to me," said Elsa, giving her friend a reassuring hug.

After a morning at the pool, Elsa was relieved to get home and find nothing had gone wrong. The stair gate was still in place and Mum said Milo had done a great job of keeping Coco entertained. Even so, she was reluctant to leave her puppy again so soon, and was the last to arrive at Ashani's.

"Sorry I'm late," she said, as she joined the others in the sitting room.

The Puppy Clubbers were gathered on the floor playing with Lulu. The little dog was cream and toffee-coloured with a patch of chocolate on her paw. Nobody quite knew what breed mix she was but her floppy ears and bristly, curly hair suggested she might have some poodle, spaniel and possibly terrier in her.

McFly, Ashani's big ginger cat, was sprawled on the sofa. Elsa noticed he didn't bat a whisker when Lulu bounded over to greet her, then padded past him back to the others. Why couldn't Juno and Lupo be like that with Coco?

Ashani beamed round at the Puppy Clubbers, then at Lulu who had now rolled over to enjoy a belly rub from Daniel and Willow. "Look how delighted she is to see you all! She'll see her puppies soon too. It's less than a week till their vaccinations, isn't it?"

"Sure is," said Willow. "We're all going together next Saturday."

Elsa pushed away a prickle of nerves at the thought of Coco getting her jabs.

"And guess what!" Jaya cried. "We're having a puppy party to celebrate their freedom in two weeks' time. Will you and Lulu be the guests of honour?"

Harper reached for her rucksack and pulled out a hand-made invitation on which she'd drawn a picture of Lulu with the puppies. "Here you go, Ashani! I made your one first."

Ashani and Lulu are invited
to a puppy party!

Date: Sunday May 6th
Time: 12 p.m.
Place: Willow's garden

Ashani beamed. "What a beautiful drawing! Lulu and I would be delighted to come! How are the puppies doing?"

Elsa was about to mention the cat situation but Harper got in first.

"I'm a bit worried about how much Minnie's sleeping. She falls asleep all the time!"

Ashani nodded. "That sounds like most puppies to me. Like babies, they sleep a LOT! Is she sleeping at night?"

Harper grimaced. "Not so well."

"That could explain it then," said Ashani. "She'll need to catch up on her sleep during the day."

Harper nodded. "Thanks, Ashani! I guess I'm just being a worrywart."

Elsa opened her mouth to talk about Coco, but this time Arlo jumped in. "Dash is living up to his name! He gets the zoomies around teatime, racing around in circles for half an hour!"

Ashani laughed. "Perfectly normal puppy behaviour."

"Peanut does too!" Willow cried.

"How's the toilet training going?" Ashani asked. "I remember your mum was worried about her new carpets!"

"Not bad. She's covered them all with plastic sheeting for now, so she doesn't get cross when Peanut has an accident, but he chews everything. We have to keep the playroom door shut so he can't get the twins' toys."

Ashani nodded. "You have to keep anything that could be harmful to your puppies out of reach, even everyday objects. Puppies are like toddlers – they try to eat *everything!*"

Elsa's eyes widened. Suddenly it didn't seem like the right time to mention the cats. This seemed far more important.

Daniel nodded. "Teddy's so greedy, we have to be extra careful."

"Yes, there are lots of human foods that can be harmful to dogs too," said Ashani.

"Like chocolate!" Jaya piped up.

32

Ashani nodded. "Any others?"

"Onions!" said Willow. "Mum told me that after she'd caught Peanut trying to steal one from the vegetable rack. As Puppy Club's Fact Finder, I vote we do some research into poisonous foods right now."

"Maybe we can make a poster to put up in our kitchens?" Arlo suggested.

"Can we borrow your laptop, Ashani?" Jaya asked.

"Of course. I'll help too."

"My vet book might be useful," Jaya said, pulling it out of her rucksack.

Lulu jumped up on the sofa next to McFly, who didn't move a muscle, while the Puppy Clubbers settled themselves at the kitchen table. They spent the next hour researching foods that were harmful to dogs. Then Harper created a poster on the laptop.

TOXIC FOODS FOR DOGS

1. Onions cause stomach problems even days after eating.

2. Garlic and chives cause stomach problems.

3. Chocolate is poisonous.

4. Macadamia nuts can affect a dog's muscles and nervous system.

5. Corn on the cob can block up a dog's intestines.

6. Avocado can cause vomiting and diarrhoea.

7. Alcohol causes sickness and damages the nervous system.

8. Cooked bones can splinter and harm a dog's stomach.

9. Grapes and raisins can cause liver and kidney failure.

10. Artificial sweeteners can cause liver failure.

Ashani printed out six copies of the poster, plus a few spares for herself and Underdogs. "Well done, Puppy Clubbers!" She looked over at Lulu and McFly, now asleep on the sofa together. "We must do all we can to keep our pets safe."

At once Elsa's thoughts flew back to Coco, at home without her. Suddenly she longed to get back to check her puppy was safe from the cats.

"You've been quiet today, Elsa," said Ashani. "How's Coco?"

"She's great," said Elsa. "Though Juno and Lupo aren't being very kind to her, and poor Coco's terrified."

Ashani gestured over to McFly and Lulu. "Those two are good friends now, but they weren't when Lulu first arrived."

"Really?" Elsa said, surprised.

Ashani nodded. "McFly was wary around Lulu for weeks. I think he felt threatened. This was his home first, after all. He was just starting to get used to her when the puppies arrived, so that was a whole new challenge! You can understand your cats being a bit unhappy, suddenly having a dog in their space."

Elsa nodded. "McFly seems fine now, though."

"Yes, he is. I used to leave a towel that I'd rubbed over Lulu near his bed, so he got used to her scent. Perhaps you could try that?"

Elsa smiled. "Thanks, Ashani, that's a great idea." She turned to Jaya. "We can add it to the Operation Friendship list."

"What's Operation Friendship?" asked Ashani.

"We're helping Elsa think of ways to make her cats more comfortable around Coco," Jaya explained.

Ashani smiled. "That's a lovely idea, but just remember, Elsa, it won't happen overnight."

Elsa nodded, feeling so much better. She would try the blanket tip when she got home. They already had the stair gate in place and she'd made a PLEASE SHUT! poster for every door in the house. Surely there was hope for Coco, Juno and Lupo yet?

As much as Elsa had loved hanging out at Ashani's, she couldn't wait to get home.

"How's Coco?" she asked her mum, when she came to collect her. "The cats haven't been chasing her, have they?"

Mum laughed. "No, the cats haven't. But Milo and I have!"

Elsa stared at her. "What?"

Mum grinned. "Coco ran into the garden with Milo's football boot so we had to chase her to get it back! She

thought it was a great game!"

Elsa giggled. "What did the cats think?"

"Not a lot. They were lazing in the kitchen! You know, I think your stair gate idea might be working," Mum said. "They definitely seem a little less bothered by Coco today."

"Ashani's suggested leaving a blanket that has Coco's smell on it near the cats' bed too."

Mum nodded. "It's worth a try."

"Ashani's sure they'll be best of friends eventually."

"Let's hope so, Elsa, for everyone's sake. There's only so much I can take."

Elsa frowned, and a niggle of worry wormed its way back inside her. What did Mum mean by that?

Chapter 3

"Quiet please, Year Four!" Mr Priest bellowed above the Monday morning hubbub. "As you know, our topic this term is 'Caring for the World Around Us'. You're going to be working on a group project – six people per group – to find out about an organization that helps animals. Any animals you like, from cats to orangutans, elephants to bees!"

He paused for the flurry of excited whispering to stop. "Next Friday I will ask each group to make a ten-minute presentation about your chosen organization. You'll have lots of classroom time to prepare for it, but you may want to do some extra work at home too. There'll be twenty house points *per person* for the winning group."

Mo put his hand up. "How will you decide the winner?"

"I won't be the one deciding!" Mr Priest replied. "You will! You'll all get a vote, and the group with the most votes will win."

Elsa craned her neck and grinned at Jaya, Harper and Willow. Arlo and Daniel gave them the thumbs up. The Puppy Clubbers would work together, of course.

"Quieten down!" Mr Priest said. "Right, once you've sorted yourselves into groups, I'd like you to spend the next fifteen minutes discussing what organization you are going to choose. Is everything clear?"

The Puppy Clubbers collected a computer from Mr Priest and gathered round a desk. Soon everyone was pitching ideas.

"It has to be dogs!" Arlo said.

"How about Guide Dogs for the Blind?" Jaya suggested as she logged in to the computer.

Harper nodded. "My neighbour would really struggle without her guide dog Patch."

"There are hearing dogs for the deaf too," Willow said. "I saw a TV programme about them."

"Wow!" Arlo said. "They must have to train hard."

"What about animal rescue charities abroad?" Daniel suggested.

"Hang on!" said Elsa suddenly. "Aren't we forgetting an amazing organization closer to home! What about Underdogs?"

Jaya grinned. "Of course!"

"Great idea!" cried Daniel, high-fiving Elsa.

"Do you think we could interview Ashani?" Harper suggested.

"And take photos," Arlo added.

Jaya nodded. "I can ask her about it later."

Elsa beamed proudly.

"Those house points are in the bag!" Willow whispered.

Elsa arrived home in high spirits, fizzing with ideas about their presentation. As soon as Mum opened the door, Coco ran to greet Elsa, barking and jumping up.

"Whoa, little lady!" she laughed. "Let me put my rucksack down!"

Elsa took off her bag and picked up Coco, giggling as she tried to avoid her excited licks. "You're such a cutie pie!" she said, wandering through to the kitchen where there was no sign of the cats.

"Hmph!" said Mum. "Cute but destructive!" She held up a pair of mangled glasses. "Look at my brand-new specs! She pulled them off the coffee table while my back was turned."

Elsa stared in dismay. "I'm sorry, Mum. Coco doesn't know what she can and can't chew."

"Well, you're going to have to teach her."

Elsa hung her head. Everything Coco did seemed to annoy Mum. "I'll make some more posters to remind everyone not to leave things in Coco's reach!"

Mum's stern face softened. "I don't mean to be hard on you, Elsa, but Coco does need to learn. Why don't you take some treats and practise a bit of recall with her before tea."

It was raining so Elsa carried Coco through to the sitting room, carefully closing the door behind them. Milo was lying on the floor doing his homework so Elsa took Coco to the other end of the room. If Coco came when Elsa called her name, she rewarded her with a treat. But half the time she ignored her!

"I think that's enough," Elsa said, after ten minutes. "I'll go and wash my hands and then we can have a cuddle."

As she was coming back, she heard a commotion coming from the sitting room. She ran in to see Milo chasing an excited Coco. "She's got my pen!" he cried.

"I left it on the floor while I went to get a snack."

"Get it off her!" Elsa cried. "She could choke!"

But Coco didn't want to be caught. She sprinted round, thinking the whole thing was a wonderful game.

Elsa kneeled down, stretching her arms wide to make a barrier, but Coco just ran round her! Milo skidded across the wooden floor in his socks, trying and failing to grab the playful puppy. Finally, he managed to corner her.

"Got it!" Milo shouted, grabbing the pen and tickling Coco under the chin to make her drop it. "Yuck, it's covered in puppy saliva!"

"What's happened now?" said Mum, appearing in the doorway. She took in the gooey pen and the guilty-looking Coco. "I think today's lesson to us *all* is not to leave things we don't want chewed in places Coco can reach!"

"Never mind us. It's for Coco's safety!" Elsa glared at Milo.

Just then, they heard some loud *woofs* through the open window. They were

coming from next door's garden.

"Pluto!" Elsa cried. Pluto was a six-month-old Labradoodle puppy. He was very cute but he was always escaping under the hedge into Elsa's garden!

"That's all we need," said Mum. "Another mischievous puppy to add to the chaos here. Let's just hope Pluto stays in his own garden today!"

Coco ran to the open window, barking happily. Then she sprang on to the sofa, racing back and forth, and was so excited she did a little wee.

Mum threw her hands in the air. "Not again!" she groaned, picking Coco up and holding her at arm's length. "Go and get a cloth, Elsa. You know, I'm starting to wonder if getting a puppy was such a good idea after all."

Elsa stared at Mum in horror. How

could she even say that? She dashed into the kitchen, taking deep breaths to stop herself crying. It felt like they were back at square one again.

Chapter 4

The next couple of days whizzed by. At school, it was full steam ahead on their presentation, and at home Elsa was busy working on her puppy party poem – and trying to keep Coco out of trouble!

On Wednesday afternoon, Jaya's mum picked up the Puppy Clubbers after school to take them to Jaya's house for some presentation planning.

"Where's Bonnie?" Jaya asked, as they walked into her house, which for once was strangely quiet.

"Fast asleep in her basket," said her mum. "Sam's at tennis, Roohi's at a play date and Hari's taking a nap, so there's nobody here to disturb her for once! Or me – it's been heaven!"

"Can we wake her?" Jaya asked.

A little bark came from the kitchen.

"Sounds like you don't need to!" Jaya's mum laughed.

A fluffy beige puppy with floppy ears scampered down the hallway and cowered between Jaya's legs. Jaya reached down and picked her up. "Don't be shy, Bonnie! Everyone's come to see you," she said, laughing.

Gently, the others reached in to stroke Bonnie but after a few minutes she wriggled out of Jaya's arms and started sprinting up and down the stairs, barking with joy!

Jaya laughed in disbelief. "I've never seen her so excited!"

Elsa watched as Bonnie dashed from room to room, with everyone chasing after her. She couldn't help feel a pang of sadness when she thought of Coco, confined to the sitting room for much of the day to separate her from the cats.

"You OK, Elsa?" Jaya asked, as she ran back into the hallway and made a grab for Bonnie.

Elsa sighed. "Yes. It's just… I was thinking of poor Coco, stuck in one room because of the cats."

"Oh, Elsa. I know it's not great, but at least Coco's safe there." She handed Bonnie to Elsa. "Here, have a puppy cuddle to cheer you up."

"What's up?" said Harper, as she and the others piled back into the hallway.

"Elsa's still worried about Coco and the cats," Jaya explained.

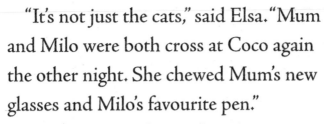

"It's not just the cats," said Elsa. "Mum and Milo were both cross at Coco again the other night. She chewed Mum's new glasses and Milo's favourite pen."

Arlo grimaced. "Oops!"

"Why didn't you tell us?" Willow asked.

Elsa shrugged. "I didn't want to sound like I was criticizing Coco. And I've been working through our list of ideas. Mum thinks the blanket trick might be working as, while the cats aren't being any friendlier, they haven't chased Coco for a while."

Jaya put her arm round Elsa. "That's good news! But remember what Ashani said. It won't happen overnight."

"Well, I hope it happens soon," said Elsa. "Mum said she's starting to wonder if getting Coco was such a good idea after all."

The others stared at Elsa open-mouthed.

"I'm sure she didn't mean it." Harper bit her lip.

Elsa caught Jaya widening her eyes at the others, as if warning them to shut up!

"Come on, guys," Jaya said breezily. "Let's go and get some snacks. Mum's made fresh samosas."

Elsa nodded, glad to think about something else for a while.

By the time they'd eaten the delicious samosas, Bonnie finally seemed to have exhausted herself, so they left her to nap and decamped to Puppy Club HQ – Jaya's garden playhouse. Jaya had put up their harmful food poster among the other dog pictures. There was hardly any wall space left!

Top Dog Daniel sank down on a

beanbag. "Right, so let's talk through our parts in the presentation. Jaya, you're going to introduce it, as Ashani's your auntie."

Jaya nodded. "I'll talk about how she started Underdogs. Oh, and I talked to Ashani and she's happy to be interviewed and for us to take some photos."

"Brilliant," said Daniel.

"Then I'll summarize the facts and figures about how many dogs the rescue centre has helped," Willow said.

Arlo put his hand up. "It's me next, talking about the different roles staff and volunteers do – and talking about us!"

"Then it's my turn," said Elsa. "I'm presenting some rehoming stories, including Maggie the chocolate lab."

"Great. I'll take photos on Saturday," Daniel added. "Then it's over to you, Harper, to make it look … whizzy!"

Harper's cheeks flushed. "No problem. I'll design the cover slide and all the headings and create the daily routine section too."

Suddenly an idea popped into Elsa's head. "Maybe…" She paused, worried it was a silly idea.

"What?" Jaya asked, intrigued.

Elsa hesitated. "Well, maybe Ashani could bring Lulu into school for the presentation. And tell her story!"

Everyone stared at her and Elsa felt her cheeks flush. "I knew it was a silly idea."

Willow patted Elsa on the back. "It's not silly. It's awesome!"

"Genius!" said Arlo.

Jaya jumped up and ran out of the playhouse, shouting, "I'll call Ashani right now!"

Elsa frowned. "Do you think Mr Priest will say yes?"

"We've had talks from people with animals before," Harper said.

Daniel nodded. "Remember when Amelia's mum came in to chat to us about being a vet. She brought a hamster into school!"

Willow hugged Elsa. "This is going to be epic!"

Arlo laughed. "Who knew schoolwork could be so much fun!"

When Elsa got home that evening she was pleased to hear Coco had enjoyed another good day.

"A few little puddles on the kitchen floor but otherwise she's been no bother," Mum said, as she welcomed Elsa home with a big hug. "One happy little pup."

As soon as Elsa opened the sitting-room door, Coco burst out of the room, leaping up and woofing happily. "I missed you so much!" Elsa cried.

"Looks like she missed you too!" Mum laughed.

With Coco in her arms, Elsa followed Mum down the hall just as Milo bounded downstairs. "Hi, sis!" he called, making a beeline for the sitting room. *Off to play his computer game, no doubt,* Elsa thought.

Mum was just handing Elsa a glass of milk when they heard an angry shout.

"No way! Coco!" Milo yelled.

Elsa and Mum came running. Milo was holding up his gaming controller, his face bright red. "Look! She's chewed right through the wire!"

"Well, where did you leave it?" said Elsa, accusingly.

Milo looked sheepish. "On the floor … but I'd only just got it out. I popped upstairs to get changed – I can't have been gone more than a minute."

Elsa felt a surge of anger. She pointed to her poster: DO NOT LEAVE YOUR STUFF AROUND!

Mum sighed. "Elsa's right." She took the controller from Milo. "We learned that lesson the other day!"

"I forgot!" Milo moaned. "I'm not used to having to share the house with a naughty puppy."

"Coco isn't naughty!" Elsa shouted.

"Calm down, both of you." Mum inspected the wire. "It's not too badly chewed. Maybe it can be repaired. Good job you hadn't got round to plugging it

in, or it could have given Coco an electric shock."

Elsa gasped and cuddled Coco closer.

"Sorry," Milo muttered.

Mum put her arms around them both. "Lesson learned … again!"

Milo and Elsa glared at each other.

"Come on," said Mum. "How about you two play with Coco, while I sort tea?"

"Fine," said Elsa. "Let's go in the garden and play fetch."

"No thanks," Milo sulked.

"Suit yourself." Elsa stormed outside and set Coco down on the grass. "Ready, Coco? Fetch!" she shouted, throwing the ball. For once, Coco did as she was asked and Elsa felt herself begin to calm down. After a few minutes, Milo appeared.

Elsa looked at him in surprise. "Want to play?"

"Woof!" barked Coco, as if in reply, making them both grin.

They threw the ball for Coco, asking her to fetch, then drop in return for a treat but after a while Coco decided Milo's old sandal was more interesting than a ball and ran around with that instead!

Milo laughed, making clumsy grabs for the sandal but Coco dodged around him easily. "You'd make a good rugby player with moves like that!"

Elsa giggled as she watched Coco run through Milo's legs. "She's far too quick for us!"

Milo picked her up and gave the puppy a cuddle. "I'm sorry I left my stuff on the floor," he told Elsa.

Elsa smiled. "And I'm sorry about your controller."

They went inside, and for once the cats didn't hiss when Milo put Coco down on the kitchen floor, or try to chase her. They just stalked off into the sitting room.

"Did you see that!" Elsa exclaimed. Milo nodded.

"I think the blanket is working," said

Mum. "The cats seem much more relaxed around her now."

As they ate their tea, Elsa felt a small ray of hope. Maybe, like Ashani said, it would just take time.

Chapter 5

"You want to bring a dog into class!" Mr
Priest's eyes were wide but Elsa noticed
the corners of his mouth twitching
upwards.

It was break time on Thursday, and the
Puppy Clubbers had stayed behind to ask
him about Ashani and Lulu. Ashani had
agreed to their plan as soon as Jaya had
asked her.

Jaya nodded. "My auntie said she would keep Lulu on the lead the whole time."

Mr Priest grinned. "Does Lulu have a speaking part in the presentation too?"

They all giggled.

"Let me run it by Mrs Handy and I'll get back to you. Now out you go, it's break time!"

The Puppy Clubbers headed outside and gathered at the playground bench.

"I hope Mrs Handy says yes," said Jaya,

crossing her fingers. "And by the way, Ashani invited us round after school next Monday to do the interview."

"Brilliant," said Harper.

"How's everyone getting on with preparations for the puppy party?" asked Daniel.

Arlo gave a cake update. "So, it's going to be chocolate cake for the humans, and my stepmum and I have found a puppy cake recipe too!"

"Really? What's in it?" Elsa asked, intrigued.

"Eggs, doggie biscuits, peanut butter, carrots and a little honey," said Arlo.

Daniel grinned. "Teddy will wolf down the lot if we're not careful!"

"Willow and I tried out a few obstacles for the agility course after you guys left last night," said Jaya. "Hoops and planks and stuff."

Willow nodded. "The pups are going to love it. I asked my dad if he has any old tyres like your sister suggested, Jaya. He's going to check in the garage."

"Have you managed to finish the invitations, Harper?" Daniel asked.

"Yes! They're in my bag. I even made some for our parents! I'll give them out at home time."

"How's the poem coming on, Elsa?" Arlo asked.

Elsa grinned. "OK … the rhyme's the hardest bit!"

"This party's going to be epic!" Willow squealed.

That evening, after playing with Coco, Elsa made sure she gave the cats some

attention too, to keep them happy. Mum had bought them a new toy – a little mouse on a piece of rope – which they loved. She did some work on her poem too, and after tea she read it out to Milo and Mum who had some great suggestions.

Friday evening was just as busy, this time with writing up some of the Underdogs' rehoming stories for the presentation. At least it meant Elsa didn't have too much time to think about the visit to the vet the next day. That night, however, she went to bed with butterflies in her tummy. Tomorrow, Coco was getting her jabs. She caught sight of Harper's beautiful party invitation on her chest of drawers and tried to focus on that happy thought instead: only eight days to go!

When her alarm clock buzzed on Saturday morning, the butterflies were back. Elsa ran straight downstairs to wake Coco and sat at the kitchen table cuddling the still-dozy pup on her knee. Juno and Lupo lay calmly in their baskets watching them.

Elsa watched Coco's tiny black nostrils flare as she breathed. "Don't worry, little one, I'll be there with you," she whispered. "It'll only hurt for a split second, then you'll feel fine." And she really hoped that was true.

When Mum dropped her off at Underdogs at nine o'clock, Elsa still felt nervous and tetchy as she, Daniel and Arlo prepared the lunch bowls.

"Slow down! You're spilling biscuits all over the place!" she exclaimed, as the boys struggled to lift the huge sack.

"Keep your hair on!" Arlo called.

"Sorry. I'm just worried about Coco getting her jab today," said Elsa.

"Me too for Bonnie," said Jaya, walking into the food prep room with Harper and Willow. Ashani was behind them.

Harper nodded. "Me three! I think Minnie will be terrified."

"Come on, guys," said Willow. "Just think about the party! One more week to go!"

"Willow's right," said Daniel.

"I've got something to take your minds

off today's vet visit," Ashani said. "We have a new arrival and we need to prepare some blankets, toys and a food rota for her. She's called Betty. Her family are moving to Australia and sadly they can't take her with them. Would you like to meet her?"

Ashani didn't need to ask twice, and for a while Elsa's nerves subsided as they found some toys and a blanket and watched Betty get used to her crate. She was so good-natured, Elsa was sure it wouldn't be long before a loving family came to give her a new home.

After lunch, Elsa gave Coco one last snuggle before Mum put her into the crate and carried it to the car for the short trip to the vet. It was only the second time Coco had travelled in it and she whimpered all the way. As soon as they arrived Elsa ran round to open the boot.

"It's OK, Coco, we're here now," she soothed.

Mum picked up the crate. "Come on. Let's get you inside."

As they walked into the waiting room, they heard Coco's brothers and sisters barking excitedly! They were all in travel crates too, but they could smell and see each other. Elsa had to admit it was exciting to have them all in the same room together and by the sound of her yipping, Coco clearly thought so too!

"What a din," exclaimed Miss Birchtree the vet, as she came out of the consulting room.

"I'm not sure this was such a good idea after all!" Willow's mum shouted above the noise.

"Me neither!" said Arlo's dad.

Miss Birchtree laughed. "Who's going to be first?"

Willow sprang up. "Let's get it over with. Come on, Peanut!"

Elsa's stomach turned when she heard Peanut's barks from the consulting room. But they didn't last long and Willow soon emerged cuddling a rather subdued puppy.

Miss Birchtree stood behind her. "Don't worry, he'll be racing around again in no time," she said.

"Can Coco go next?" Elsa said, her voice coming out a little wobbly. "I want to get it over with too."

Miss Birchtree gave her a warm smile. "Come on through."

Mum picked up Coco's crate and Elsa slowly followed.

"Right, Elsa," said Miss Birchtree. "You take Coco out of the crate and give her a cuddle while we take some details. How's Coco doing?"

Elsa giggled as Coco snuffled into the sleeve of her jumper. "She's great!"

"Settling in OK?"

Elsa shot Mum a nervous look.

Mum gave a tight smile. "Well … we have two cats so that's been problematic."

Elsa's eyes widened. Did Mum just say Coco was a problem?

"Cats can be tricky when there's a new pup on the block," said Miss Birchtree.

Mum nodded. "We've had to install a stair gate to stop them chasing her."

Miss Birchtree nodded. "Great idea."

"Then of course there's the chewing…" Mum continued. "My brand-new glasses and Elsa's brother's game controller so far."

"They weren't Coco's fault," Elsa blurted out, feeling outraged on Coco's behalf. Why was Mum dwelling on the bad things? Everything had been great the last couple of days, hadn't it?

Mum looked a little taken aback at Elsa's outburst.

Miss Birchtree smiled reassuringly. "I can see you care very much about Coco, Elsa." She gave the puppy a little stroke behind her ears. "Have you tried anything else?"

Elsa nodded. "I have a list. We've put one of Coco's blankets next to the cats' beds at night, to try to get them used to her scent."

"Really good idea. It can take weeks, even months, for cats and dogs to settle with each other." Miss Birchtree glanced at Mum. "As for the chewing, Elsa's right – anything you leave in reach of a new puppy is fair game."

Mum shot Elsa a brief smile. "I know. It's just a bit … frustrating."

"Where are the cats and Coco sleeping?" the vet asked.

"Coco's in the kitchen where the cats used to sleep as it's the warmest room," said Mum. "And we moved the cats' beds into the hall."

"Aha!" said Miss Birchtree. "That could be part of the reason the cats resent Coco. They feel she's taken their place. Perhaps you should move their bedding back to where it was and put Coco's crate in another warm place."

Elsa nodded. The vet could be right.

"And don't force them to be best friends," Miss Birchtree went on. "Just make sure they all get plenty of attention and, little by little, let them into the same room – under supervision." Miss Birchtree reached for Coco. "Right, shall we get this pup vaccinated? Then, in a week or so, you'll be able to take her out for walks!"

Elsa handed Coco over and screwed her eyes shut. She didn't want to watch. "All done!" said the vet a few seconds later, as Coco let out a loud bark of disapproval. Elsa felt her eyes fill with tears of relief. She immediately picked Coco up and cuddled her in close. "I'm sorry, Coco. I know that hurt, but it's to keep you safe."

Mum put her arm round Elsa and

ruffled Coco's ears. "You OK, Elsa?"

Elsa nodded but she wasn't really. Aside from poor Coco getting jabbed, she felt all churned up inside about Mum telling the vet Coco was a problem. Did she even like Coco?

"Well done, Coco, for being so brave." Miss Birchwood smiled. "And well done, Elsa, too. I bet the next time I see you, Coco and your cats will be great friends."

"I hope so," said Elsa, frowning at Mum.

Mum nodded. "Me too! I'm worn out!"

Back home, Mum shut the front door quietly and put Coco's crate down in the hall. After a few minutes of whimpering when they first got into the car, Coco had

quietened down and when they opened the boot she was fast asleep, clearly exhausted by her visit to the vet.

"That wasn't so bad, was it?" Mum whispered.

Elsa shrugged.

Mum looked puzzled. "Is everything OK? You hardly spoke on the way back."

Elsa took a deep breath. "It's just … well, you seem to be so cross with Coco the whole time. You told Miss Birchtree she's a problem. And she's not! She's the best puppy in the world."

Mum stared in surprise. "Oh, Elsa, I don't think Coco's a problem. I said the situation was problematic. It's difficult with the cats, of course, but I'm sure we'll get there."

Elsa stared at Mum, unconvinced.

Mum picked up the cats' cushions.

"How about we do what Miss Birchtree suggested and move the cats' beds back into the kitchen. We can leave Coco's crate here next to the radiator in the hall?"

Elsa nodded and followed Mum through to the kitchen. "I just want you and Milo to love Coco as much as I do," she blurted out, tears pricking her eyes.

Mum put the cushions down and pulled Elsa into a hug. "We do love Coco! Though nobody could love her as much as you. I'll try to be more patient from now on. After all, it must be confusing for Coco too, coming somewhere new with two strange animals who haven't been the most … welcoming!"

"Exactly!" Elsa hugged Mum back. "All Coco wants is to be their friend."

"Fancy a hot chocolate?" said Mum.

Elsa grinned. "Can we have squirty cream and marshmallows?"

"Absolutely. I think we both deserve it!"

As Mum filled the kettle, Juno and Lupo stalked into the kitchen. As soon as they spotted their beds back in the kitchen, they jumped on them, purring in delight! Elsa sat down on the floor beside them, dangling their new mouse toy for them to try to grab. After a few minutes, both of them settled on Elsa's knees.

"Look at you two being all cuddly!" She laughed. "Is this a thank you for having your sleeping place back? I love you both, you know, and from now on I'll make sure I show you that, so you don't feel left out."

Later, at bedtime, Elsa was delighted
that Coco seemed perfectly happy to cosy
up in her new spot too. "Do you think
I should wait beside her crate, until she
goes to sleep?"

Mum smiled but shook her head. "Coco will be fine. And if she does make a noise, we'll hear her."

Elsa took one last look at Coco. "Sleep well, little one," she whispered before heading upstairs, crossing her fingers that Coco would have a good night.

Operation Friendship was starting to work, Elsa thought, as she drifted off to sleep. She was still feeling a tinge of crossness with Mum but it only made her more determined than ever to prove that Coco was definitely *not* a problem and was as much a part of their family as Juno and Lupo.

Chapter 6

BEEP! BEEP! BEEP!

Elsa woke with a start at the sound of
her alarm. Seven o'clock. She strained to
see if she could hear anything. Silence.
Had Coco really slept all through the
night in her new spot? The vet had
warned them the puppies would be very
tired after the jabs. She crept downstairs
and peeked under the blanket covering

the puppy crate. Coco was curled up at the back, snuggling her cuddly unicorn dog toy.

Elsa stifled a giggle as the puppy let out a sudden snore. She was dying to get her out for a cuddle, but Coco looked so peaceful she left her to sleep and went to get a glass of milk. In the kitchen, Juno and Lupo were happily sprawled on their cushions. Elsa gave them both a stroke then sat down at the table with her notebook. Now was the perfect time to work on her puppy party poem.

Twenty minutes later she was just trying to think of a word to rhyme with fluff when she heard a little yip from the hallway. Coco!

Elsa plucked the puppy from the crate and sighed happily as Coco nuzzled her little black nose into the crook of Elsa's arm. A moment later she began to wriggle around.

"Uh-oh!" Elsa hurried towards the kitchen. "Morning wee time!" She put Coco down outside and to her surprise, Juno and Lupo wandered straight past, without a single hiss or back arch! Elsa smiled to herself. She had a good feeling about today.

When Mum came downstairs Elsa and Coco were playing fetch. "I've just had a text message from the leisure centre. Today's swimming lessons have been cancelled as the pool filter's broken."

Elsa gave a thumbs up. "That gives me more time with Coco and to finish my

poem. Oh, and I need to do some work on the presentation."

"You have a busy day ahead!"

Milo wandered in, yawning. "Morning!"

"Want to play fetch with me and Coco outside?" Elsa asked.

Milo nodded. "Let me just grab some breakfast."

Mum poured some milk into her mug. "Once I've done the online shop, I'm going to take my coffee upstairs and start that book we're reading for Book Club. It's not often we get a lazy Sunday morning, is it?"

Milo wolfed down two bowls of cereal in half the time it usually took Elsa to eat one, then joined Coco and Elsa outside in the sunshine. Elsa was trying some recall training. It was hit and miss.

"Coco! You have
to at least try!"
she cried, as the
puppy ignored
her command
again in favour of
chasing a butterfly.

"Listen!" Milo interrupted. "Can you
hear that?"

Elsa heard scrabbling behind her and
spun round. The hedge was shaking.

"Pluto!" Elsa and Milo chorused, as a
small black nose poked under the hedge,
followed by a curly blond head.

For a split second, Coco stared at Pluto
then pelted over, barking a greeting at the
top of her voice, as if unable to believe
he was actually here! The next moment
the new friends were chasing each other
round the garden at breakneck speed,

jumping over one another, yipping and woofing, then rolling around in the grass before starting all over again!

Elsa ran after them. "I thought Harvey had blocked up the gap under the hedge!" she shouted.

"So did I!" Milo cried, as Pluto ran through his legs.

"Grab Pluto!" Elsa hollered, as she lunged towards Coco, who sprinted straight past her. "They shouldn't be mixing yet! It's not even a full day since Coco had her jabs."

"Elsa!"

Mum was standing at the back door, holding up a book with a large chunk chewed off the corner. "What on earth's going on?" she asked, watching Milo zigzag across the lawn after the puppies.

"Pluto got under the hedge again and now we can't catch them!" Elsa cried.

Just then, there was a loud "MIAOW!" and Juno and Lupo darted past Mum, sprang down the steps and joined in the chase, gaining on the puppies who were now tearing round in a wide circle.

"Shoo!" Elsa yelled, waving her arms at the cats as Milo made another unsuccessful grab for Pluto.

The cats ignored her and made a beeline for Coco. Juno pounced in front of the puppy and before Elsa could pluck her out of the way, the cat made a swipe at Coco, catching her on the nose. The puppy yelped in shock and stopped in her tracks.

"You horrid cat!" Elsa yelled, grabbing a whimpering Coco up into her arms.

"Is she OK?" cried Milo, who had finally managed to catch Pluto.

"I don't know!" Tears ran down Elsa's cheeks as she held her puppy close.

Mum came over and checked Coco's
nose. "She's alright. It's just a scratch."

"Do you think we should take her
to the vet?" Elsa sobbed. "It might get
infected and…"

"She's fine, Elsa, honestly." Mum gave
an exasperated sigh. "So much for a

relaxing Sunday! I was coming outside to tell you that Coco somehow got to my book before I did!" She held up the chewed book again.

Elsa stared in dismay. This morning she had been so full of hope. How could it all have gone wrong again?

Mum put an arm round her. "Come on. Let's take Pluto home."

Isla, the eldest of next door's children, opened the door and stared at Pluto in surprise! "How on earth…"

"He got under the hedge again!" Milo explained, handing the puppy over to Isla.

Isla's sister and brother, Rosa and Frankie, appeared behind her, followed by their mum, Kate. "Not again! What a scamp! I'm so sorry!"

Mum gave a tight smile. "No problem. I know just how much trouble puppies can be. Every day I find myself wondering why on earth I agreed to getting one!"

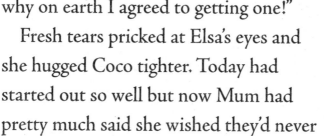

Fresh tears pricked at Elsa's eyes and she hugged Coco tighter. Today had started out so well but now Mum had pretty much said she wished they'd never got Coco!

Kate smiled sympathetically at Mum. "Believe me, there were times when I thought the same about Pluto during the first few months. But it does get easier! Do you fancy a coffee?" she asked. "I'll put Pluto in his crate so Coco can have the run of the garden."

Mum gave a frazzled smile. "That would be lovely."

Milo ran through to the back garden with Isla, Rosa and Frankie but Elsa lingered in the doorway, nuzzling Coco's fur. She just wanted to take Coco home but Mum ushered her inside.

"Come on, Elsa," Mum said. "Let's join the others."

In the garden, Milo, Frankie and Isla were already bouncing on the trampoline while their dad, Harvey, tapped pegs into the bottom of some wire fencing. "He's managed to dig underneath and loosen it," he explained to Elsa. "That dog is a regular escape artist!"

Elsa managed a smile and put Coco down on the grass.

"Coco's so cute!" said Rosa, coming over. She was the same age as Elsa but at a different school. "I can't wait till she and Pluto can play together."

"Me too..." Elsa smiled. "Although right now I think Mum would happily

98

give her back to the rescue centre!"

Rosa looked shocked. "She wouldn't, would she?"

Elsa glanced over at Mum who was sitting at the garden table with Kate. "She's finding having a puppy pretty stressful," she explained. "What with the cats attacking Coco and Coco chewing everything in sight, she seems to think Coco's more trouble than she's worth."

Rosa frowned. "I remember my mum tearing her hair out when we first got Pluto! He'd be awake half the night and he had so many accidents all over the house. He once pooped in the bedroom and he chewed *everything!*"

"At least you didn't have two unfriendly cats in the mix too," said Elsa.

"I'm sure they'll get used to each other," said Rosa. "How's the training going?"

Elsa shrugged. "Mixed!"

Rosa grinned. "Do you want to do some now? Pluto's recall was awful at first, then one day it just clicked."

Elsa nodded and fetched Coco from over by a lavender bush. Then they stood at either end of the garden holding treats.

"The key is to make sure your voice is firm and the command sound is the same each time," Rosa explained. "Coco can't understand words but she can understand the tone of your voice."

Rosa demonstrated, then Elsa had a go, raising her voice for *fetch* and lowering it for *drop*, rewarding each successful attempt with a pat and a treat. It actually worked ... sometimes! By the time Mum had finished her coffee, Coco had definitely made some progress.

Back home, Mum set Milo and Elsa to work peeling the vegetables for lunch while she had a shower. Elsa still couldn't get Mum's words out of her head: *I find myself wondering why on earth I agreed to getting one.*

"You don't think Mum would send Coco back to Underdogs, do you?" Elsa asked Milo, as she reached for another carrot.

Milo shot her a puzzled look. "What are you talking about?" he said.

Elsa sighed. "Well, yesterday she told the vet things were problematic with the cats and Coco, and today she told Rosa's mum that she sometimes regrets getting a puppy. I'm worried I'll come home from school one day and Coco will have … gone!"

"Don't be silly. Mum loves Coco. So do I."

Elsa shrugged. "Really? Then why does she never tell Coco that and why is she so grumpy all the time?"

"Having a new puppy in the house is hard work," Milo reasoned. "I think Mum's just been so worried about Coco and the cats, she hasn't had a chance to enjoy her." He paused. "I guess I haven't

102

helped, forgetting to shut doors and leaving my stuff out." He looked over at the cats who were busily cleaning themselves. "Hey, didn't the vet say you should try having all three of them in the same room for a short time?"

Elsa nodded.

"How about we give it a go once we've done these veg? I'll grab some toys to distract Juno and Lupo and you can keep Coco occupied. With a bit of patience and time they'll be best mates before you know it."

Elsa wasn't so sure but she was glad of her brother's support. Sometimes Milo wasn't so bad after all.

Chapter 7

On Monday morning, Elsa hurried into
the playground, and was soon relaying
yesterday's drama to the Puppy Clubbers.

"... then Juno swiped at Coco and
caught him on the nose! You should have
heard her yelp!"

"Is she OK?" Jaya cried.

Elsa nodded. "Yes, but I was so upset.
Thankfully things calmed down later.

Milo and I even tried having Coco and the cats in the kitchen together and it was actually fine. They just ignored each other – no hissing or chasing!"

Harper grinned. "Phew!"

"But what a drama!" said Arlo.

"Is everyone still OK to come to interview Ashani after school?" Jaya asked, as they headed inside.

Her friends nodded.

"Let's hope Mr Priest says it's OK for her to bring Lulu in," Harper said.

Daniel nodded. "He must have an answer from the head by now."

Sure enough, at break time, Mr Priest asked the Puppy Clubbers to stay behind.

"So, Mrs Handy has spoken," he said, looking serious. Then his face broke into a grin. "It's a yes. Lulu can be here for your presentation, Jaya."

"Yes!" Willow cried, whacking Harper on the back.

Arlo high-fived Daniel and Jaya. "Whoop! Whoop!"

A smile spread across Elsa's face. Her idea might just give them a chance of winning those house points!

After school, Jaya's mum met them at the school gates to walk them to Ashani's.

"Mrs Handy said yes!" Jaya cried, as soon as Ashani opened the door. "You can bring Lulu in on Friday!"

Ashani beamed. "That calls for celebration cookies, I think!" She led them to the kitchen table, where a plate of cookies and a large jug of water were already waiting.

"Tuck in!" said Ashani, as Lulu trotted in to say hello.

As soon as they'd had the cookies it was time for the interview. Chief Scribbler Jaya was taking notes along with Elsa. Daniel had brought a voice recorder and they had each prepared a question.

Willow launched straight in. "So, Ashani, how did Underdogs start?"

Ashani smiled. "Ever since I can remember, I've always loved dogs. Then, ten years ago, I saw an article in the local paper about a dog that had been abandoned in the park and was starving. It made me so sad, I really wanted to do something to help. I got in touch with some dog rescue centres and I worked at a lovely one for a couple of years, but it was an hour's drive away. There weren't any nearby. That's when I had the idea of setting up my own!"

"When did Underdogs open?" Jaya asked.

"Nearly eight years ago. Since then, it's gone from strength to strength. We started out with a handful of dogs. And now we've rehomed over five hundred!"

"Wow!" said Elsa. "Why do the dogs get brought to you?"

"Well, sadly some of them have been abandoned or mistreated, or their owners have had to let them go because they're moving house or going abroad. Every dog needs lots of love and patience."

"It sounds super busy," said Arlo. "You must have lots of people working for you?"

Ashani shook her head. "Actually, I only have two full-time members of staff. Everyone else is a volunteer! As a charity, any money we raise is put straight back into the centre so we can achieve our aim – that every dog who comes to us can go on to a happy life in their forever home."

As the interview went on, Elsa's admiration for Ashani grew. She was listening so hard that at one point she forgot she was meant to be taking notes. She had no idea just how much work it took to run Underdogs. It made her feel proud to be part of it, even in a small way.

Lulu wandered over to Ashani and nosed her knee. Ashani reached into her pocket and gave Lulu a treat. "You're certainly an Underdogs success story, aren't you, Lulu?"

Elsa reached over and gave Lulu a scratch behind her ears.

Arlo smiled. "We have a lot to be grateful to Lulu for, don't we?"

"Yes, it's thanks to you, Lulu, that we all have our puppies," said Daniel.

Jaya gave Ashani a hug. "And you, Auntie. Without you there'd be no Underdogs!"

Ashani blushed a little. "My pleasure. After all, what fun would Puppy Club be without real-life puppies?"

Chapter 8

With only three days to go until presentation day, the Puppy Clubbers had each been putting the finishing touches to their section. Elsa had spent Monday evening typing up her part with Coco curled up in a ball on her lap! By bedtime, the *Underdogs' Success Stories* was looking great.

On Tuesday, they had all gathered

at Elsa's house after school for a run-through. As they piled into the sitting room to play with Coco, Juno and Lupo snuck in too. But rather than chasing after Coco, they jumped up on to the windowsill and curled up for a nap.

"I can't believe how calm the cats are around Coco compared to last time we were here!" Jaya said.

Elsa beamed. "I know. They've stopped hissing at her now, though I wouldn't leave them in a room on their own just yet."

"It sounds like Operation Friendship is doing a good job!" said Arlo.

Elsa nodded. "I don't want to jinx it, but I think it's working ... finally."

"Fingers crossed!" said Mum, who was trying to connect her laptop to the TV so they could practise the presentation in front of their slides, just like they would in class. "Bingo!" she called, as the title page of their presentation appeared on the big screen.

Everyone clapped. "Let's go!" Daniel said. "Jaya, you're up first."

"Mum, will you time us, please?" Elsa asked. "We're meant to fit it into ten minutes."

"Sure!" Mum smiled. "Ready, Jaya?"

Jaya nodded.

"OK. Begin!"

As Elsa ended the presentation the Puppy Clubbers broke into fits of laughter. Willow had got some of her facts muddled up and Arlo had forgotten to mention the role of Suzy, Underdogs' assistant manager, but it was sounding brilliant.

After more practice on Wednesday and Thursday, everyone was pretty much word perfect. She might be biased, but Elsa thought they were going to smash it.

On Friday, Elsa left for school feeling happy and for the first time she didn't worry about leaving Coco behind. That afternoon they were all going round to Jaya's for a play date, the sun was shining and the puppy party was only two days' away! There was a lot to be excited about.

In class, the groups drew lots to see what order they would go in, and Elsa was glad when they picked to go on last.

Everyone had clearly worked super hard on their presentations, and Elsa learned loads from each one. Lydia's group focused on an orangutan charity in Borneo, Ahmed's group talked about a local hedgehog hospital, Stan's group had researched a donkey sanctuary and Liv's group explained all about a cat rescue centre. Each charity sounded equally wonderful. And they weren't the only group to incorporate an animal guest! Ahmed's uncle, who volunteered at the hedgehog hospital, brought in a very sleepy hedgehog who'd been injured on a road. Elsa was so engrossed in what she was hearing she almost forgot they had to do their own presentation too!

When Mr Priest called their group up, Elsa's tummy began to churn with nerves. Could they really do as good a job as everyone else? The competition was tougher than she'd imagined. Once Jaya began their introduction, though, she spoke with such confidence that Elsa's own nerves flew away and by the time it came to her section, she was more than ready. In fact, it went really well!

Then, at last, it was time for their big surprise! The *piece de resistance*, as Mum had called it – Ashani and Lulu's grand entrance!

"Now you've heard a lot about Underdogs' founder Ashani, and we also talked about Lulu, one of the rescue dogs who now lives with her," Jaya began. "Well, now we have a treat for you…"

There was a ripple of excitement as Jaya looked towards the door. Everyone followed her gaze. They'd managed to keep their special guests a secret from everyone but Mr Priest, so when the door opened and Ashani and Lulu walked in, their delighted classmates erupted with cheers! Elsa beamed. This had been *her* idea after all!

As Ashani told the story of how Lulu had come to Underdogs, you could have heard a pin drop. At the end, they showed photos on the big screen of all Lulu's puppies from the day they were born right up to now. *Coco's grown so much in that time*, Elsa thought!

"Can we please say a huge thank you to Ashani and Lulu," said Mr Priest, as everyone clapped.

Once the children had calmed down, Mr Priest said, "I think you're going to have a tough time voting. All your presentations were brilliant! And while Lulu – and Spike the hedgehog – were of course adorable, do not be swayed! By all means vote for a group that had animals on show, but do so because their presentation was your favourite, not because they brought in cute guests!"

Everyone laughed.

"Now, if you could write down the name of your chosen group and hand it to me, I'll count the votes while you get your coats and announce the winner before you go home!"

It took Year Four much longer than usual to get ready, as they were all so busy chatting about each other's presentations. Eventually, though, they filed back into class.

"It's been a very close-run competition," said Mr Priest. "Only one point in it! But the winners are ... Jaya, Daniel, Arlo, Willow, Harper and Elsa, with their presentation on Underdogs rescue centre. Twenty house points to each of you for your different houses!"

"YES!" Willow shouted. She punched the air then pulled her friends into a group hug. Elsa looked round at her smiling classmates who were all applauding. Ashani stood at the back, beaming. Even Lulu looked as though she was smiling. They had actually won!

"This calls for a celebratory ice cream!" said Ashani, as they went out into the sunshine. "I know I told Jaya's mum I'd take you all straight there for your play date, but how about we go via Swirls?"

"Yay!" everyone chorused. Swirls did Elsa's absolute favourite: one scoop of bubble-gum ice cream and one of mint choc chip in a sprinkle-covered cone!

She linked arms with Jaya and Harper as they headed off. This was turning into the best day ever!

Chapter 9

"We won the house points!" Elsa cried, as soon as she came through the door that evening. Jaya's dad had dropped her home.

"That's brilliant news!" Mum called back, as she appeared from the sitting room holding an armful of unravelled toilet paper!

"Oh no!" Elsa cried. "Coco?"

Mum nodded, but for once she didn't look cross. "Not just Coco, though! She had a little help from her friends. Come and see!"

Puzzled, Elsa left her rucksack in the hall and followed Mum into the sitting room. Coco was sitting on top of a small pile of toilet roll, looking very pleased with herself, while Juno and Lupo batted the rest of the roll back and forth. Elsa couldn't believe her eyes. "But … what happened…?"

Milo laughed. "I forgot to close the stair gate when I went to get a drink and the cats wandered through. Meanwhile, Coco must have escaped to the bathroom and snuck a loo roll from the basket. When I came back they were playing with it together, rolling around in it all, having the best time!"

Elsa beamed at Milo, then at Mum, who was smiling. Had Operation Friendship finally worked? Suddenly, before she could stop herself, Elsa burst into tears.

Mum dropped her armful of loo roll and ran over. "Elsa! What's wrong?"

"It's just … I've been so worried about everything, with the cats being mean to Coco, and all the chewing and weeing and escaping and everything, and I was…"

Elsa paused for breath.

"What?" Mum asked.

"I was worried you would send Coco back to Underdogs!"

"Oh, Elsa!" Mum said, pulling her into a hug. "I would never do that!"

"But you've been so cross whenever something went wrong," Elsa wailed.

Mum's eyes widened. "Elsa, I'm so sorry. I hadn't realized how stressed out I was. I knew it would all be fine in the end. I'm sorry I didn't make that clear."

Elsa stared up at her through blurry eyes. "Did you?"

Mum nodded. "Of course!"

"You have been pretty tough on Coco, Mum," Milo muttered.

Mum nodded. "Yeah, maybe I have. I'm sorry, Elsa. I wish you'd told me how you were feeling. I love Coco. It's just a big change, that's all. And it's been a lot tougher than I imagined. But I promise, Coco is here to stay!"

Elsa hugged Mum tightly.

From over on her loo-roll pile, Coco gave a cheery bark.

Elsa giggled. "Coco, come!" she called. And to everyone's surprise, the puppy ran straight over!

"You see! She's finally learned her own name!" Mum said, laughing. "From now on, Elsa, if you're worried about anything, please talk to me, OK?"

Elsa nodded. "I will, Mum, I promise!" she said, scooping Coco up into her arms. "Did you hear that, Coco?" she whispered. "You're here to stay."

On Saturday morning, Elsa wasn't the only one at Underdogs who found it hard to keep her mind on a task. Everyone was so excited about tomorrow's party!

"My stepmum's gone to get the ingredients while I'm here," Arlo said. "We're making both cakes this afternoon."

"Remember, we're coming to drop the agility course stuff off straight after we finish here, Willow," Jaya said.

128

Willow nodded. "Mum and Dad are doing a big shop this morning too. Mum said she'd make us puppy party bags to take away! One for the pups and one for us!"

"Awesome!" said Arlo.

"I've been practising the face painting on my sister," said Daniel. "How's the poem coming on, Elsa?"

"Almost there!" she replied. She was a little nervous about what the others would think but she still had time to make some last tweaks.

When Sunday finally dawned, Elsa opened her bedroom curtains and looked out on to a cloudless May sky. Her stomach did a little flip of happiness. Puppy party day!

There was no swimming again, as the pool filter was still broken, and by midmorning, Elsa had practised reading out her poem at least ten times and was desperate for it to be 12 o'clock. Mum had said they could walk round to Willow's and Elsa could hardly wait. It was going to be Coco's very first walk!

"How long to go now, Mum?" she asked, hopping from foot to foot.

Mum laughed loudly. "That must be the seventeenth time you've asked! Why don't you go and get yourself and Coco ready and we'll leave in a bit. It's only a ten-minute walk, but as it's Coco's first one, it might take a lot longer."

Elsa didn't need telling twice. Up in her room, she pulled on her favourite T-shirt and paw-print dungarees, then fixed her hair in two plaits tied with puppy-shaped bands. She ran back downstairs to give Coco one final groom before putting on her brand-new sparkly red collar.

"Puppy-party ready!" she said, holding Coco up to the mirror.

"Time to go!" Mum called.

"Yippee!" Elsa cried, carrying Coco to the front door where Milo helped clip the matching red lead to her new collar. Coco could clearly sense something exciting was happening and started whizzing up and down the stairs, barking madly!

"Hope she calms down for the walk," Milo said, laughing.

Once they were all out on the street, Elsa couldn't have felt prouder. Finally, she was getting to walk her very own puppy! Coco was in doggy heaven and stopped to sniff every wall, tree and lamp post, and do a little wee now and again, which Elsa and Milo thought was hilarious. Every noise and movement was a source of amazement to Coco, and

Elsa had to keep a firm hold of the lead to make sure she didn't pull too much. Elsa tried to make her sit every time they reached a road, but Coco was too excited for that! As Mum had predicted, what should have been a ten-minute walk took over double the time because Coco was so distracted, but Elsa didn't mind. It had been a success. She finally felt like a proper dog owner!

"Are you ready, little one?" she asked Coco, as they walked up the path to Willow's front door. "Time to be reunited with your puppy brothers and sisters … and your mum! This is going to be a day to remember!"

Chapter 10

"Elsa and Coco have arrived!" Willow's mum called out, as they walked into the back garden.

Willow and Jaya were already there, checking the agility course. "Hooray!" they cried and ran straight over to hug Elsa.

Bonnie and Peanut were happily chasing each other round the lawn and

Coco began to bark, straining at the lead to join them.

"Shall I let Coco off?" Elsa asked, a little unsurely.

Willow laughed. "Of course! She'll be fine. There are no holes under our hedges!"

Elsa unclipped Coco who dashed straight over, yipping loudly, and all three pups began rolling around together!

Elsa watched in delight.

"They've missed each other!" Jaya said.

"Look at them sniffing each other's bottoms!" Willow laughed. "Why on earth do dogs do that?"

Elsa shook her head. "I have no idea!"

"What's so funny?" came a voice from behind.

Elsa spun round to see Arlo holding Dash's blue lead. Dash was long-legged and lean, with tightly curled reddish hair.

136

He was straining to reach his brother and sisters and began to bark loudly.

"I'd unclip him if I were you!" said Arlo's dad who was standing behind him holding two large tins. "Now where shall I put these cakes?"

"This way," said Willow's mum, leading him towards the kitchen.

The excitement and noise levels shot up again as Harper and Minnie, then Daniel and Teddy arrived. Teddy was bigger than his siblings, golden brown with curly hair like Dash. Minnie looked tiny in comparison.

"Isn't it amazing that such different-looking puppies can come from the same litter," said Elsa.

Jaya nodded. "I guess it's the same for humans – brothers and sisters don't always look alike either."

The six pups whirled around everyone's feet and just as Elsa thought they couldn't get any more excited, Ashani arrived with Lulu. For the next few minutes, pandemonium broke out! Lulu's six puppies bounded over, nuzzling in and jostling for their mum's attention. As the smallest of the litter, Minnie was left scrabbling at the back, but she didn't give up and was soon in the thick of it, alongside her brothers and sisters.

"She might be little, but she's feisty," Harper said proudly.

"Coco and Bonnie are holding their own too!" Jaya cried.

Elsa grinned. "Girl power!"

"Right, kids," said Elsa's mum. "What are we doing first?"

"Cake!" the Puppy Clubbers shouted.

Arlo's cake was decorated with tiny, fondant-icing models of Lulu and her six puppies. It tasted delicious! The cake he'd made for the puppies was in the shape of a large bone. Arlo's stepmum cut it up and put it in six bowls. Teddy wolfed his down in one munch. Coco only sniffed at hers, but before Elsa could take it away, Teddy ate that too!

Daniel shook his head. "Told you!"

Jaya laughed. "Right, poem time, Elsa, then we'll do the agility course after that!"

Elsa nodded, suddenly feeling a little nervous.

She waited for everyone to gather
round, then took a deep breath and in her
loudest voice she read:

It started with Lulu, a poor little stray,
Rescued by Underdogs one winter's day.
But after a while, to Ashani's surprise,
Six pups would appear,
each a different size!
The biggest was Teddy,
a boy and quite greedy.
Then Dash, who turned out to be
terribly speedy.
Two sisters next… Bonnie:
a cream ball of fluff.
Then chocolatey Coco,
so cute, but quite tough!
Next Peanut, a patch of brown fur
on his paw,
Then finally Minnie, the smallest of all.
They came to our houses.
Six small puppy stars.
And now, none of us can believe
that they're ours.

Everyone cheered and as the Puppy Clubbers surrounded Elsa, Mum beamed and gave her a thumbs up.

Next, it was time for the pups to try the agility course. First up was Coco, who ran round the hula hoops instead of going through them. Then it was Dash's turn but he was too busy sprinting

around to try any of the obstacles. Bonnie and Teddy chased each other the wrong way through the mini slalom but Peanut got the hang of it straight away and even jumped over the hurdles brilliantly. Last to go was Minnie, who got halfway along the course before curling up for a nap inside one of the tyres!

After that the puppies had a snooze, so the Puppy Clubbers painted each other's faces in their club code names. Daniel was Greyhound; Elsa Cockapoo; Jaya, Collie; Willow, Springer, Arlo, Labrador and Harper, Dalmatian.

"I hope you're not all going to start running around like puppies too!" Willow's dad laughed.

Then of course that gave Arlo the idea for them all to have a go at the agility course!

All too soon it was time to go home.

Ashani hugged everyone and Lulu gave each of her pups one last nuzzle. "Thank you for a lovely puppy party."

"You must come again soon." Willow's mum smiled. "Just maybe not all at once!"

"What a brilliant party," Mum said, linking arms with Elsa and Milo, as they headed home with Coco. "I'm exhausted, though. How about we order pizzas and watch a movie?"

"Yes, please!" Elsa and Milo cried.

Poor Coco was so tired that Elsa had to pick her up and carry her the last few minutes. As soon as they got back she fell fast asleep on the rug in the sitting room, while Elsa and Milo ordered pizzas and flicked on the TV to look for a movie.

"Can we watch *Cats and Dogs?*" Elsa asked. It was her all-time favourite film.

Milo laughed. "Sounds like the perfect choice for this house!"

Half an hour later, the doorbell rang and the house was filled with the mouth-watering smell of pizza. Mum brought through the pizza boxes and some drinks.

Just as they'd started eating, Juno and Lupo trotted in.

"Oops," said Mum. "I forgot the stair gate."

"Uh-oh!" Elsa jumped up as the cats drew close to Coco and Mum readied herself to shoo them away, but to their amazement the cats had a little sniff around the puppy, who remained fast asleep, then they wandered off and curled up next to each other.

Milo grinned. "I hate to say I told you so, little sister, but didn't I say these three would be great mates?"

Elsa smiled. "And I hate to say it, big brother, but for once you were right!"

Mum reached for Elsa's hand. "You see? Everything's going to be OK."

Elsa looked at Coco, fast asleep without a care in the world. "You know," she whispered, resting her head on Mum's shoulder. "I think it finally is!"

Puppy Club Personality Quiz: which Puppy Clubber are you most like?

1. What's your favourite pastime?
a) watching movies
b) gymnastics
c) baking
d) reading
e) drawing
f) football

2. What's your favourite colour?
a) red
b) blue
c) pink
d) purple
e) green
f) orange

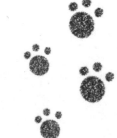

3. Which adjective best describes your personality?

a) kind

b) energetic

c) laid-back

d) confident

e) thoughtful

f) sporty

4. Which dog breed is most like you?

a) Cockapoo

b) Springer spaniel

c) Labrador

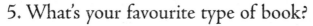

d) Collie

e) Dalmatian

f) Greyhound

5. What's your favourite type of book?

a) fantasy

b) comic strip

c) cookery
d) non-fiction
e) graphic novel
f) funny

6. What is your favourite kind of music?
a) pop
b) hip hop
c) rock
d) dance
e) soul
f) rap

7. What's your favourite subject at school?

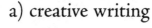

a) creative writing
b) PE
c) cookery
d) science

e) art
f) geography

8. What would be your favourite trip out?
a) cinema
b) picnic
c) restaurant
d) science museum
e) art gallery
f) swimming

9. What's your favourite type of movie?
a) mystery
b) action
c) comedy
d) drama
e) musical
f) animation

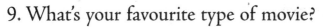

10. What would you like to be when you grow up?
a) nurse or doctor
b) sportsperson

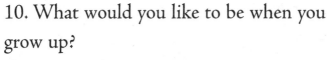

c) chef
d) vet
e) illustrator
f) teacher

Results:

Mostly As – you're most like... Elsa!
With the shy but kind-hearted nature of a cockapoo, you will always be the first person to look out for your friends!

Mostly Bs – you're most like... Willow!
Absolutely bursting with energy that could rival a Springer spaniel, there's never a dull moment when you're around!

Mostly Cs – you're most like... Arlo!
Like Arlo you are outgoing, creative and friendly. You may be a little clumsy at times but you're always open to trying new things!

Mostly Ds – you're most like... Jaya!

With your confidence, determination and excellent people skills, you can do anything you put your mind to – like convincing your parents to get a puppy!

Mostly Es – you're most like... Harper!

From making birthday cards to designing Puppy Club posters, you are overflowing with creativity, just like Harper!

Mostly Fs – you're most like... Daniel!

As a walking encyclopedia you are super smart, but your love for physical activity also makes you super sporty, just like Daniel!

How to draw a puppy

1. Start by drawing a bean shape for the puppy's body.

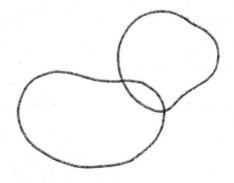

2. Add a round shape for the head.

3. Give your puppy a long, waggy tail.

4. Add his two back legs.

5. Draw two sausage shapes for the puppy's front legs.

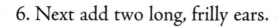

6. Next add two long, frilly ears.

7. Now rub out the overlapping lines with an eraser.

8. Give him a friendly face. And finally add a collar!

Catherine Jacob loves writing stories for children and also loves dogs, so *Puppy Club* is a dream to write. She lives in Yorkshire with her husband, three young children and a Labradoodle puppy. Many of the *Puppy Club* puppies' escapades are based on real-life events!

Catherine is also passionate about the environment and as a TV reporter, she has travelled around the world, including the Arctic and the Amazon, but she's happiest back at her writing desk, drinking tea and eating biscuits.

Hailing from Hampshire, Rachael Saunders
is an illustrator with a passion for storytelling
and character design. Her distinctive, bright
and joyful work spans the worlds of children's
literature, animation, product design
and handbags.

When she's not creating beautifully whimsical
illustrations, she can be found playing tennis
or getting lost in the New Forest while
walking her dog.

Look out for the next Puppy Club book
coming soon…